Genesis
in the
Inferno

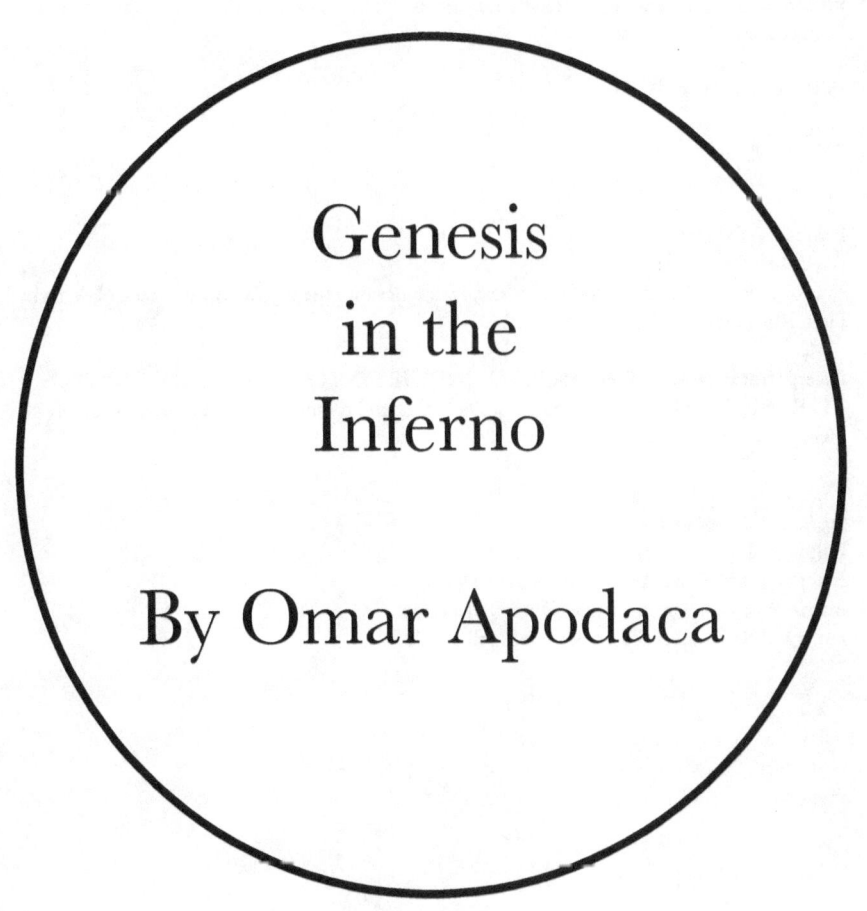

Genesis
in the
Inferno

By Omar Apodaca

ISBN: 978-1-7334365-7-1

www.omarapodaca.com

Story: Omar Apodaca
Editor: Erik De La Cruz
Front and Back Cover Design: Javier De La Cruz
Interior Book Design and Layout: Erik De La Cruz
Front and Back Cover Illustrations: Johnathan Sek

Contents

Chapter 5 — Purgatory

Chapter 6 — Salvation

Chapter 7 — Genesis

"The quest for certainty blocks the search for meaning.
Uncertainty is the very condition to impel man to unfold his powers."

— *Man for Himself*, Erich Fromm

Dedicated

To my parents. For working nonstop to provide the best for me, As I've grown older, I've realized the true magnitude of your obstacles to raise our family. Making sure that we had the best opportunities to flourish. With that in mind, I will not take you for granted. Thank you for everything that you do for me, even to this day. I love you.

To Erik. For always believing in my potential as a writer and person. You saw my gift early on and urged me to write a book before I even considered that a possibility; knowing very well the type of impact it can have. I think it's fitting that you played an instrumental part in the completion of this work. I appreciate your help, as well as for always being there for me.

To Alexander and Tito. I could not have asked for better brothers. We're each so different, yet we complement each other so well. You have both played a fundamental role in my development. I'm very grateful to have you both in my life.

To those who are living in anguish. I hope my book is able to inspire you and help you keep going through the difficult times.

Author's Note

I intensely and painstakingly crafted this book, in large part for you. It has an intricate storyline, which I believe is best enjoyed by reading it in order from start to finish.

Although this is a work of fiction, a lot of the topics are based on real events. Personal moments that include adventures I've embarked on, heartbreaking experiences, and catalysts that have led to self-transformation. All of which have forged me to become the person that I am today.

I published my life and sorrows. My burden has been lifted, I can finally let go.

I can begin anew as I give these words to you.

If my book inspires, motivates, and pushes you to become the person you envision yourself as, then I will have accomplished my purpose in writing it.

The genesis begins now.

Love,
Omar Apodaca.

Chapter 1
Banishment

Parallel Universe

A portal opened to realize my life's greatest dream,
Yet I missed the call to take the spring of reaction,
Blinded, paralyzed, restricted by fear,
Forever lamenting my lack of bravery and bravado,
Now I live in a steady state of shame and regret,
This is my biggest blunder.

If I could defy the laws of physics,
I would go into a parallel universe,
Where I willingly ventured into the wormhole,
Alas, there I find Valhalla.

There I'm living the life of my wildest imagination,
Playing in front of a crowd of tens of thousands of jubilant fans,
The maestro at work with the ball at his feet,
Being the decisive factor by controlling the tempo,
And winning the match.

I returned to my own world forlorn,
Living a bleak and dreaded existence,
For I am the antimatter to my counterpart realizing my true calling,
In that alternate world where I was meant to reside,
If only I had taken that athletic scholarship,
To play the sport where I'm the best sport possible,
Since in living my calling I purge myself of mental toxins,
Revealing the glee that's my greatest inner treasure chest,
If only I had answered that coach's email to activate the portal,
I'd be on my path to become the best.

Detour

It has been a wild journey traveling with no end in sight,
Climbing the sand dunes while skipping the tunes,
My skills as an accurate archer are tarnished,
For I have lost sight of the bull's-eye,
These repeated setbacks have me feeling defeated.

The new target in sight has me reaching with all my might,
Pulling back the bow to transform possibility into action,
Potentially landing on my greatest ambitions,
Kinetic and magnetic are my aims,
In desperate search of the magical prize,
Released in liberation as I'm launched.

The bow bows down in reverence,
Nock leads to my inevitable rise,
No longer a walk as the fletching straightens me out,
The proper shaft prevents me from splitting up,
Arrowhead is now more potent than ever.

In mid-flight I'm knocked off with a collision,
Spinning around like particles in nuclear fission,
With a different trajectory I land in another space,
Wondering how this occurred with a bewildered face,
Now to embark on a new mission starting from scratch,
In search of the bull's-eye as I remove the eye patch.

Back Burner

So many highways to construct,
Numerous skills to perfect,
Some of my greatest passions,
On the back burner they are placed,
To fulfill necessary obligations.

I lock up my checkerboard circle,
Along with my low-key yet forte friend,
Pencil and paper in the pen of constricted classless cubicles,
As I complete my societal sentence,
And make my contribution to this rat race.

Soon I shall be reunited,
With hobbies galore,
They say ignorance is bliss,
But not with your leisure amiss.

Trailblazer

I'm the type of individual,
Who has always marched to the beat of his own drum,
Preferring seclusion to blind devotion,
You may think this disposition is mainly glum,
And to be quite honest — that assumption is partially correct,
My surroundings encompassed by turrets,
When actually I'm just protecting my base,
Annually planning for my next big move to make.

Freedom is something that comes with a price,
Constructing a new path is not for the serfdom,
Although a troublesome process,
I no longer choose to dwarf myself,
For it is better to lose it all while building a new trail,
Than to blandly walk a finished path,
And wielding little autonomy,
Just to follow the masses,
While clouding the vision with murky glasses,
The only allergy I've developed is one to mediocrity,
Which is why I battle and battle with such ferocity,
I'm not tech-savvy,
But I'm on a quest to 3D print an empire from scratch.

Expedition

On a tour of many cities,
I feel like a circus act,
Except there are no tricks or stunts to perform on my behalf,
Adventuring as a pirate on land,
Without the looting or being contracted under a monarch,
These landscapes leave a mark on me,
That is real impressionism,
Mannerisms change from spot to spot,
Leading preconceived notions to rot,
This is the removal of the red dot sight,
To morph into a pacifist during the exploration of the Pacific,
An assimilation of cultures to adopt a practice of acceptance,
Dissolving the abomination of political divisions,
To learn to share this invaluable planet we inhabit,
Instead of hiding inside of holes like a rabbit.

Mama Shasta

A warm and welcoming mother,
With the power to freeze time at your will,
You are my heaven on Earth,
As I tread around your bosom in my infancy,
I am wisdom-fed with your arctic milk,
You put me in my place when I act out of order,
Forcing me to fix my faults and flaws,
Now I am aware of the feline's claws,
You catapult me from a newborn into a grown tree,
Now I sprout into the sky astute, untamed, and free.

Computer Plant

Nature is the head honcho,
Worthy of worship and admiration,
Seamlessly weaving complexity and simplicity together,
You are the only one capable that can create perfect geometry,
That shapes the flowers and celestial bodies with pinpoint precision,
Containing a mystique that can mend, like no other,
No matter how much destruction occurs,
You regenerate life when all seems lost, most of the time,
An unlimited diversity of organisms is created and nurtured by your grace,
You are the best shrink around,
Stripping away the seemingly permanent conditioning from my mind.

I could spend an entire lifetime,
Next to your patient presence,
And not feel like I have wasted a single moment of it.

Tranquil

I peek around every corner,
Emulating the movements of the owl,
To avoid getting pierced by the tranquilizer,
Getting seduced by the sedative is not an option,
Regulating my internal waves,
Steering through the turbulent waters to stay on course,
This is my method of functioning,
Conservation of fuel for the right mission is a must,
It is crucial to safeguard against the lust of danger,
One reckless move could even sink the Titanic,
Which can be averted by regulating panic,
Composure can preserve the composition,
As regulation can preserve the reputation.

Astronaut

Houston... we have a problem,
I have stepped into unfamiliar territory,
My lungs never cease to be strained,
It must be the gravity of the situation —
Of inhabiting this green and blue sphere,
Not even meditation is a permanent aid,
It just becomes like medication.

Wherever I step feels like the surface of the moon,
Even upon undertaking the most trivial tasks,
A glitch ripples throughout me,
Filling me with a need to repeat said task,
Again, and again, and again, and again,
Completing every single day,
Feels like accomplishing a perilous space mission,
I feel the need to freeze in motion,
While everything just orbits around me,
Don't call me a coward,
Just because I cower,
The constrictions of living wear me down.

Maybe I didn't prepare enough for this Earth expedition,
Or perhaps I wasn't strong enough to begin with,
If you see me staring off... spacing out,
It's because I'm an astronaut,
However, instead of a conquest of the stars,
Across the galaxy and beyond,
I'm aiming my sights on Terra,
The third pearl from the Sun in this solar system,
And whether or not I am ready,
I'm not holding back.

Shinobi

I'm not of the shadows,
But I operate well in them,
Silence is my natural mode of default,
From my speech to my movements,
While summersaults are the mode of default in the courtyard,
I'd rather have the element of surprise on my side,
To keep those around surmising,
Often scaring people with my cat-like stealth,
No wonder it's so easy for me to get overlooked.

I wouldn't trade away these powers even for vast rewards,
Since they make me who I am,
Being so low profile that people think I'm in limbo,
Others think I'm spineless for this,
I'd rather have you refer to me as Your Highness,
Who diligently serves the masses,
Embodying the code of the samurai,
Blended with the covert art of the ninja.

Hyperloop Escape

My exile begins here.
Leaving behind everything,
The misfortunes and missteps are too much to handle.
I'd like to leave without the slightest trace,
But I leave a note out of consideration.

In the new venture the grass is meaner.
I become a servant of my pride,
So I prefer to hide away like a stowaway.
With all my possessions tucked in a suitcase,
I anticipate the worst and fear for the best.

It took me less than a mere 3,600 seconds,
To realize that I had acted brashly.
Like a child from the third grade.
I guess there's no shame in admitting my mistakes.

No matter how fast I travel,
Or how far I traverse,
My problems will always stick beside me,
As the adhering takes me away from here.
Unless I yank them away from my bare skin.
A removing of the burdensome bandage.

Mattress

I feel very depleted and exhausted,
It is my natural state in this waking realm,
Safety and comfort are things that always elude me,
Can't help but dread that wicked forces are colluding against me,
My one true sanctuary through thick and thin,
Is crawling underneath the bedsheets safe in my skin.

If sleep is the cousin of death,
Then I must be half-dead,
Since my preferential residence is in the REM cycles,
No amount of stem cells can cure this never-ending *dis-ease*,
This enticing harmony sucks me in,
Making me never want to wake up again.

It gets so bad that when I wake up,
Sometimes I spend hours stationed to the outpost of my bed,
Dreading the battleground that lies beyond my spongy encampment,
This must be some variant of PTSD,
It's like I have to be tethered to a bungee cord,
To be forced to complete my daily tasks;
Can't help from being like an empty flask,
Searching for an ethereal liquid,
Perhaps the fourth state of matter,
To energize me up with fulfillment to the core.

Backpack

The alarm jolts me awake with a sudden outburst.
I grab a heap of clothes as I race to put them on.
Then I get the car keys and slowly advance through the traffic.
Upon arrival at the train station I fight for a parking spot,
Like a hawk spotting its next meal.
The train ride is full of sullen faces, foul stenches, and crowded spaces.

After getting off the stop I take the shuttle to campus,
Full of worry for the day ahead.
I grab a quick bite to tame my starving stomach,
Then go to the most crowded spot on campus: the library.
Seeking to emulate the speed of a skilled typist,
I forge a B paper with C- effort and A+ haste.
I turn it in class and get a slap in the face from a pop quiz I did not prepare for.
Some lecturing ensues, then downtime before my next classes.
I roam the campus like it's a ghost town,
Feeling like I belong in another setting, another era.
I arrive at my beloved temple, the stadium.
And daze off into the distance,
Desperately wishing for a change in setting.

I rush off to my last two classes for the day,
Surviving my taxing marathon session.
Cramming nearly six straight hours of classes,
As if I were cramming for a major test.
Nothing significant transpires.
Just PowerPoint slides, so-called group projects,
and the professor's lessons that mainly regurgitate from the book.
As soon as the last class is dismissed, I race to the shuttle line,
And barely get on board as I transport to the station.
During the train ride I'm dozing off,
Struggling to stay awake so I don't miss the transfer point and my stop.
I get off, circling the parking lot to find where I parked earlier today.
The drive home is one of the smoothest parts of my day,
Making me feel as if I'm in control.
I only have four more years to put up with this.

Solitaire

Solitude has always been my trustworthy companion,
Whether I feel like a champion celebrating with a champagne bath,
Or an incessantly somber screwup,
Obsessing over a way out of this laborious labyrinth.

I'd much rather be the leader of a 1-person pack,
Than relinquishing my autonomy to a disastrous group,
Where I just run circles around the ringleader all day,
Resulting in nothing but dismay.

With the passing of the seasons,
My fangs only keep getting sharper,
So I need to take advantage of them,
While being cautious of my vantage point,
In relation to the full moon,
For it can alter the mood of women and men,
Just like it fluctuates the position of the tides.

I have to tidy up my act,
And prepare for this long and cold winter ahead,
To survive the taxing timberland,
Where laxness can lead to sudden death.

Meager Nomad

I need to gather myself together,
Or I will end up becoming the hunted,
Excluded from the tribe for a premature burial,
Lack of a club leads to a ride for rations,
Rationality can cause commotion — a la Cro-Magnon,
I stand tall even under the presence of a Neanderthal.

A wise man, a magus, and a scholar,
Though he bears no gifts with him,
He uses the map up above to head east,
With only a beard and rugged clothing,
He searches for his abode,
Wretched yet refuses to wither,
The only imprints he has,
Are immediately covered by the dust,
The prince has a price to pay.

Chapter 2
Execution

Confidence

Self-efficacy is the way to go,
It is the only way to know,
When we are bred amidst a farm of uncertainty,
The end result is a collection of wilting crops,
Leaving us lopsided by default,
So we can't really fault the stars,
Be alert of artificial hormones that are injected into your psyche.

What does confidence entail?
I see it as confiding in yourself,
Even if no one else in the world does,
That is the true definition of confidence to me.

The wills of individuals have:
Led to groundbreaking inventions,
Advanced our civilization,
And even forged entire empires.
Understand that the underdog is often the victor,
Feasting off the sweet nectar of success,
As he or she contains hectares of belief,
That water the soil,
Creating an abundance of harvest,
Their inner treasure chest,
Leading to the discovery of El Dorado.

Puppet Master

An accomplished prospect on the way up.
This exceptional talent becomes a target.
When the guard is let down,
The ventriloquist seizes the marionette's strings,
Tugging on the muscle fibers.
The puppet master can now control the puppet's actions at will.

The doll now is clumsy.
Movements are sporadic.
It starts to wreak havoc.
Creating new foes on the horizon.
Intentionally spoiling golden opportunities.
Engaging in reckless acts.
Until the mannequin ends up wrecked.

The puppet master hysterically chuckles,
As the strings are dropped,
Piled atop the immobile corpse.
Now flying off in search of the next target.

Was this due to black magic?
Or a snowball effect?
Through a simple mistake?
Or some negative karma?
Who knows...

The Fall

The trials and challenges were a total fail,
Now I'm stuck paying tribute upon being vanquished,
Lapped and surpassed on all ends,
More to it than just staying in my lane,
Better to faint of exhaustion than disappointment,
The truth that's hardest to swallow:
That I didn't give it my all.

Although I ended on a high note,
It was not enough to reach the baseline requirement,
I never developed to reach my prime,
Or at least anywhere close to it,
The greatest pain is the way I let myself down,
The entanglement of ambitions and fantasies are severed,
Cutting my very lifeline,
Toiling and foiling away,
Causing an extinction of the reverie.

So Be It

If I'm carrying a boulder,
And it's so heavy,
It ends up crushing me on the spot,
Then so be it.

If I'm walking on a bridge,
Made of decrepit pieces of wood,
And the plank ends up breaking,
Plummeting me to my demise,
Then so be It.

If I'm in the Sahara and I chase mirages of oases for days,
Until I collapse of dehydration,
Buried under a sandstorm,
Then so be it.

If I end up shooting for the constellations,
Yet I just miss exceeding the Earth's escape velocity,
And end up burning into a crisp on the descent down,
Then so be it.

If I'm taking a stroll in the park,
And a meteorite strikes me down,
Splattering me into a thousand pieces,
Then so be it.

Dominance

There is a yearning that I contain that nothing else can emulate,
A severe burning that amps my spirit up to the third-degree,
It is to dominate on the *fútbol* field like few before ever have,
To dribble past defenders at ease as if they were just cones,
And have my spectacular skills on showcase,
Giving chills to the spectators that reach their bones,
To dish passes out to my teammates with laser precision,
Setting up goals by serving assists out on a silver platter,
Moving with the utmost agility across the green plane,
Scoring at will from both inside and outside the 18-yard box,
In a way that leaves the opposition in futility.

The complete player is what I aspire to be,
Number 10 emblazoned on the back of my jersey,
Not showing mercy to whomever I'm up against,
Flowing my talents on the giant rectangle,
Without consciously knowing the exact process,
Due to countless hours to forge the requirements,
A meticulous build of ability to perfect the sport,
To rewire the neural networks and deliver results with ridiculous effect,
Excelling with such beauty everyone thinks I'm a video game hack,
Revolutionizing tactics with my mere attack,
I have a knack for this.

Windows of Opportunity

Alertness is of paramount importance,
For incidents that are your shot towards glory,
Usually happen at an instance,
And missing them is like putting that one-way ticket to the promised land in the shredder.
See the total view of the panorama,
For failing to notice your shot,
Ends up filling your system with free radicals.

It's about spotting the windows of opportunity,
That warp in and out of your reality like tachyons.
These zones of realization also vary in length,
With casual opportunities being miles long,
While once-in-a-lifetime opportunities,
Are infinitesimally small in comparison,
Whether a few meters wide or even inches.
Keep in mind that smaller zones travel at faster speeds,
Like subatomic particles traveling at nearly the speed of light.
Therefore bigger fish to fry,
Involve quicker decision-making and pinpoint execution.
It takes superb marksmanship;
To capture the most valuable windows of opportunity.
Learn to capture your chance,
Before it fades away,
Leaving you to clean heat-treated sand for the rest of your life.

Kotinos

Competing in the domain of the five rings,
Shouldering an entire country on my back,
Among the most elite athletes of all,
With a suffocating pressure that would crumble most.
A lifetime of preparation,
While avoiding to have the time of my life,
Yet actually relishing it,
Even more than superficial gratification.
Who am I kidding?
There's no place where I want to be more in the entire cosmos than here.
This is my moment to shine,
I was born for this.
Watch out,
I'm going for the gold.
Nothing less will suffice.

Inquisition

This... means... everything to me.
More than any reward, monetary value, or possession.
It is the sole purpose of my being.
Realizing this yearning,
Will bring me unparalleled joy,
Even if every other aspect of reality is decimated.
That's how much elation,
Accomplishing this will bring me.
If this is that important to me,
Then why did I do nothing?
It's a question that baffles me to this day.

Divine Companions (Part 1)

As a teenager I received the best Christmas present,
It was not a fancy toy or a splendid game,
But a snow-white dog that among our house drew fame.
His small frame did pack a punch,
As his feistiness made him difficult to tame.
He brought much-needed unconditional love to my life,
Possessing a zest and innocence that made everything around him seem fictional,
He always managed to steal the show like a Hollywood star.

The years went by as the calendar pages scrolled,
Impressively enough this resilient dog did not fold,
He still played and ran as a mighty beast,
Never turning down the slightest opportunity to feast.
Some of my most treasured memories involve taking him on our intimate walks,
It was much more than just simple exercise,
They helped me put my worries away,
And brought simple happiness to my hectic days.
Even as he was losing his teeth through age, his childish essence remained.

One afternoon I took my dog out for one of our routine walks,
He had his usual expression of pure ecstasy as soon as I grabbed his leash,
Jumping about like he had springs attached to his legs.
This was no ordinary stroll,
For upon turning around the corner we encountered someone walking two Germanic canines,
Before I could even process what happened those two mighty dogs latched onto mine,
Biting him at opposite ends with the grasp of a crocodile.
My spirit was in pure agony as it was a torturous sight to watch,
I was unable to rescue my dog from this onslaught,
Being accompanied by an absolute feeling of helplessness.
Finally the other owner was able to restrain his animals,
But by then it was too late.
My poor pooch lay on the floor motionless like a rag doll,
Yet somehow he mustered the strength to stand again.

I carried my dog home since he was too wounded to effectively move,
And accompanied my family as we took him to the vet,
With great hopes that he would survive.
However, they were instantly tarnished,
As the worst possible news came to pass.

The doctor said he had slim odds of surviving,
And the surgery was too expensive to pay for,
So the only alternative was to give him one last peaceful rest.
My brother and I said our final goodbyes to our little furry trooper,
Tears violently pouring down our faces,
And right before my dog died — even he had tears in his eyes,
It's almost like he knew what was to come,
And he was grieving too due to parting ways with his human family.
Seeing my dog take his last breath,
And lose his life the way he did,
Was one of the saddest moments of my life,
In a storybook already littered with great misfortunes, sorrow, and heartbreak.

It was an event that forever left a mark on me.
Especially since I could have avoided the tragic outcome,
A deadly error to take him down that route,
And leave him exposed to the other dogs,
As a result he took a fatal beatdown.
A part of my innocence was killed off that day along with my dog,
As he walked out of my life when I needed him most.

Farewell

My pride has been enveloped by the dirt,
Leaving me hurt and in tatters,
Climbing a bunch of ladders,
That lead me to nowhere,
Without the cash to pay the fare.

The promised land I seek,
Is a path only my heart knows how to reach,
Teach me how to bypass this frigidity,
It seems like I have reached absolute zero,
My particles are just motionless,
Can't break the achievement barrier,
As I just wait and wait,
Letting it all fly by,
Leading me to believe this is a sci-fi,
The results seem out of my control,
A comeback that has slipped my grasp.

Bad Enough

I'm stuck here deeply dissatisfied with myself,
The objectives on the rearview mirror remain unmarked,
The work that matters most is put to the side,
While the meaningless work takes up the main act.
No one to confide my greatest ambitions and aspirations with,
For this is not my true purpose,
Looking back on all this... the only person to blame is me,
Perhaps I didn't want it bad enough.

Fear is injected into every cell of my body,
Every square inch of my energy field,
Leaving me immobilized like a mummy.
I've dug myself in the largest hole,
Without the use of a shovel,
Nothing to do now but shrug.

It has taken me many years to realize this —
That to reach the pinnacle of success,
In any endeavor whatsoever,
It has to be something you're willing to die for!
To reach the league of the greats, that's needed.

They say happiness leads to success,
But I don't buy into that concept.
It may be a half-truth, with no half-life,
But happiness alone isn't the equation to the formula,
Since pure joy leads to total acceptance of the situation around,
And therefore stagnation.
I believe it has to be a hybrid,
Of joy for the task or project at hand,
Along with a total loathing of the incapacity of reaching one's full potential,
Since in the root of that loathing lies a source of love,
Making it as holy as an ignorantly elated state.
It has to be something you want bad enough.

Trusted Steed

A crafty farmer has multiple animals at his disposal,
The ace up his sleeve is a splendid stallion,
Though he does not truly care for the trusted steed,
Only seeing him as another tool to utilize.

The trusted steed is malnourished,
And supplied with murky water,
Locked up in the cell of a stable,
Only seeing the sunlight when the man needs a ride,
The horse is painfully branded with hot steel,
Also being disciplined with the owner's signature whip,
He flaunts his possession among the agrarian community.

Farmer embarks with trusted steed,
On an inspection of his vast property,
At the outskirts of his acres,
The workhorse is fed up,
And thrusts the owner upon the ground,
Then gallops away,
Paying back every harsh treatment endured,
With one swift act of revenge,
The man is badly injured from the fall,
Encounters a bandit,
And meets his end with cold hard steel.

In-Body Experience

You are the most marvelous thing I will ever possess,
Yet neglecting and taking you for granted is so easy to do,
You are more complex and intricate,
Than the greatest device that can ever be made,
With regeneration capabilities that defy logic,
What a super gift I have been bestowed.

Yet I malnourish you,
And sometimes don't even feed you at all,
I don't rest you adequately,
Pompously rejecting the notion of a biological clock,
I seek for methods of escaping you,
Instead of embracing you,
As the sole reason I am alive in this world,
I treat you like garbage,
And wonder why I'm getting ineffective results.

An entire universe of microscopic organisms operates on my behalf,
The ultimate act of caregiving,
I can't call a babysitter to take care of you,
I must do it myself,
And learn to cherish this sacred vessel, that I'm housed under.

Capital Punishment

The decision has been made,
I'm seen as a threat,
So I'm being taken out,
Though the stakes are high,
I will not be burned at the stake,
Despite everything hanging on the balance,
I will not be hung,
Although I'm public enemy number one,
I will not be shot down by a firing squad,
The final verdict is a beheading,
A crowd gathers to watch,
As they place me on the guillotine,
The blade reaches the apex,
The rope is let go,
And the rest is history.

Chapter 3
Inferno

Village

The ville can nurture you,
Or it can stain you,
Marking you as a villain,
It can serve to cultivate,
Or turn into spoiled goods,
Cropping you out of the picture,
A highway that serves as a passageway of commerce,
A pickaxe that brings fame to the region,
A shovel where it's all ditched for the hope of sustenance,
The three pillars of predestination,
Turning into acts of desecration,
Explanations that turn into elaborations,
As the boring is exterminated,
And the crime earns the dime,
Which is used to buy excitement,
No more returning to the slum,
Where the crumb is for the dumb.

World Stage

Ever since I was a little kid I've dreamt of the limelight,
To play at the highest level on the world stage.
Instead I'm left playing pickup games with a bunch of beginners,
And now I'm left blindsided and in pure shock of what I've done wrong,
This shouldn't be the life I'm living right now,
I feel like a hostage in this reality with no rescue in sight,
No sum of ransom can save me, however large.
A part of me has died and I am living every day pulling the carcass of this dead weight,
I sit and ponder whether it's too late and my ship has sailed,
It would be easier to end my life because I know I have failed,

But I swear on my soul what has kept me alive is my rage and drive!!!
Along with my pride and refusal to quit by taking the easy way out.
I've been robbed and cheated of my destiny,
I must dig to the ends of my inner self to find the strength that I need,
For no one can turn my life around but me.
I wish I had a redo button to start all over again,
But I have to make do with what I have and improvise the situation.
Perhaps my biggest mistake was holding back;
Letting others influence and dictate my own path.
This is still a story in the making,
I'm sure you can tell by looking at the pain in my eyes I'm not faking,
In a world so cold and cruel — all we have is our dreams,
So hold on tight, and don't relinquish them,
Or risk losing yourself in the process.

"Create your life or die," is the motto.
Don't shy away from the stage you set for yourself,
Be it a global stage or a local one.
Otherwise you'll be living in regret like me,
For we all have a calling to take,
So seize it and take control of the reins.
Leave it all on the playing field or you will be subbed out,
Watching dismally on the sideline as the game ends,
There goes your shot, wallowing in defeat,
And that's a sting that will never go away,
I know from personal experience.
So I advise you to learn from my mistake,
To keep your life from going astray.

Channeled Rage

With a wrath that can inflict fire upon the heavens,
An ensuing bloodbath is seen all around,
Canoeing past the river of despair,
An excess of flare that leads to a pure explosion,
This is the devastating power that rage has.

But... if that anger can be properly directed,
With a clear directive in mind,
This force can lead to magnificent results,
With a magnitude that shakes you to the core,
This is no mere folklore,
As it is evident in rocket ships,
That use a great portion of their fuel,
To lift off against the force of gravity,
In a violent yet regulated burst,
Instead of collapsing to form a gigantic ball of flames,
The ship powerfully propels into outer space,
Where the momentum keeps it moving forward in the vacuum,
In a victory lap around the edges of the galaxy.

It takes great precision to utilize the capability of fury,
It's a tightrope walk to either fabulous results,
Or a declining slope towards an engulfing trench,
Where the fallen are cast into oblivion,
With a corruption that's darker than obsidian,
It's a steep price to pay,
For misusing one's emotional gunpowder.

Chronos

I am desperately disputing with Chronos,
To turn back the clock for me.
The ticks on the watch leave me full of itches and aches,
An infestation I cannot halt or even slow down.
It is an arms race to surpass those tiny little arms,
That move in one direction nonstop,
Without skipping a beat,
Or even showing signs of exhaustion.
All this begging is to no avail.
For father is strict and stern,
Yet always fair.

There are theories that he is an illusion,
Yet he somehow manages to control the fabric of our reality.
All bodies traverse through this wave,
And eventually the surfboards show signs of decay.
Though the iron will and fortitude can slow the weathering down.
That is the advice pops left me.
Although impossible,
This is the closest one can get to turning back the clock.
And even if devices to venture back the continuum exist,
That does not mean the body can be everlasting,
For father works in tandem with the Grim Reaper.

Civil Dispute

Blades are clashing during Crusades,
Spearheaded by *holy* intentions,
To capture sacred relics and hold the city down,
Shots are fired throughout the land,
Some heard around the world,
Innocents are slaughtered by "friendly fire,"
Cannonballs splash across the seven seas,
Spanish galleons in search of treasure at all costs,
And mutinies overthrow even the most tight-knit and noble crews,
The sky is overwhelmed with dogfights,
Crafts and pilots plummeting on sight,
Raining projectiles, metal debris, and bodies,
Resources are extracted from the ground,
Leaving it dry and barren,
To fuel mechanized societal powerhouses,
Casualties are mere byproducts,
The weapons and devices change,
But the end result remains the same.

Tech Bars

There is the temptation to sell my soul in cryptocurrency,
But I will only end up imprisoned in an augmented reality for life.

Cycles

This planet is a giant washing machine,
For everything moves in a vicious cycle,
With no concern or sympathy,
For the hamsters running the wheel eternally.

We're born running around our mother's womb,
Just to stay afloat.

We come into the world,
Conditioned in schools,
Where the curriculum is recycled every year.

As we grow, we tread around the conveyor belt that is Earth,
Riding around endlessly in loops.

Once we finish school, we complete the circle of life from our parents,
Repeating their steps by forming a family of our own.

We're scolded for even taking a breather from running our hamster wheel...

For our energy fuels the micro-cosmos of society.

We find a job to survive and not thrive,
Prostituting our skills for money,
To move us around and around the 3D board game.

Finally, we reach the end of our lives,
And complete the 360-degree revolution,
For the trillionth time.

After dying, we chat with Death herself,
And she says, "You did your job as wheels,
powering the system with your vital forces,
now go back there and do it again."

Directional Mayhem

I thought I had it all mapped out.
Every single route, turn, step, and stop.
Failing to take into account:
The delays, dismay, taxing relays, derailing.
Now I end up as a measly spot,
Being crossed out without a second thought.
The cartographer sees me as a nuisance.
Entropy has destroyed my trophy life.
It is the way the mechanism functions.
The mere cog in the apparatus,
Is eventually worn out by the abrasion,
Done in by splints,
Splintering the base.
Disarray powers the play.

War of the Moments

For as long as our species has been around,
We have been constantly partaking in skirmishes,
Committing atrocious acts,
In a capricious manner,
Cursed with a *mideath* touch,
Because everything we touch,
We end up destroying,
Mother Nature can attest to that.

This may be due to our chaotic lifestyles,
Guerilla warfare is in every household,
For we are constantly battling with moments,
Where we relentlessly struggle with inner peace,
Tearing ourselves into pieces,
With no true intermission between our tasks,
With no room for replenishment,
Where even the tiniest slipup,
Can lead to death,
Even in the comfort of our home.

The margin of error is slim,
Where catastrophic mistakes,
Have a reverberation like clapping into a canyon,
Rome wasn't built in a day,
But the dinosaurs were quickly dispatched by a space projectile,
There is no set or clear path to win this war,
Mindfulness may be our greatest ally,
But even then the innumerable variation of tactics,
Makes the deciphering of codes an impossibility.

Gluttony

I'm starving and need to grab a bite,
The appetizer is appealing and delicious,
But leaves me wanting more.

As the main course arrives,
I succumb to my survival instincts,
And vigorously devour the plate in front of me.

I'm full and satisfied,
But can't help myself,
When I see the plate of dessert teasing me,
After forcefully stuffing it down inside my stomach,
I feel like my insides are about to burst.

I make this culinary pattern my routine,
And before I know it,
I'm nearly breaking the scale.

This leads to complications,
And before I know it,
I rest six feet under the grave,
Where the maggots are eating me.

My hunger is what kept me alive,
The problem was when I let greed overcome that hunger,
And ended up paying the ultimate price,
I stopped doing the things I had to do,
Complacency snuck through the window,
Impulse snuck through the back door,
Then together they ended up destroying my house.

Gorgon Fury

Coils wrapped around your head,
A pristine and deadly look you possess,
With a forked tongue that draws one into your words,
Your bloodstream is littered with venom,
Malignant from the inside out,
Yet your outer appearance is impeccable and lovely,
With your innocent glare,
You intend to turn me into granite,
Little did you know,
That I am completely unaffected,
Since my heart is already made of stone.

Corporate Reign

We sure have come a long way from our nation's history,
From indentured servitude to sharecropping,
Now to having corporate shares in the unicorn hopes,
That we strike it rich,
From banking our years on 40 acres and a mule,
To getting golden handcuffs along with a 401k and a pension,
Our dilemma used to be oppression based on ethnicity,
Now it's social classism,
And the widening wealth gap we have to fret about,
The 1% shoving the lower and even middle classes,
Into a further sinking liquefaction of poverty,
Where the housing crisis forces a multitude of homes into liquidation,
Inanimate companies are given more rights,
Than most of the human population,
And are treated better in the courtrooms,
These entities are committing *planetcide*,
Giving the environment a relentless beatdown,
Threatening our very existence,
But the only thing that matters to these corporate empires is the bottom line,
Where artificial green paper is given the ultimate value,
And dollars and cents override common sense.

Workaholic

Forget the bottles of beer,
Or the shots of liquor,
I suppress my dreary thoughts,
And disappointments from unfulfilled aspirations,
With overtime shifts and working around the clock.

Forget the aspirin,
I just dive into monotonous and dreadful tasks,
Putting on a mask to complete the job,
Playing a specified role for so long,
That I forget who I truly am.

I fold and can't help but sob,
As I just accept the automatized motions,
Operating like a robot,
Allowing the reboot to alter my operating system,
Leading to a predestined path to falter,
Where I can't even find the solution by praying to an altar,
A career path leading to a dead end,
I don't have the strength to fend for myself,
Seeking to mend a fantasy land that was vaporized into ashes,
And scattered into the wind.

Jaded

If it appears like I'm a jagged edge,
That's due to being pushed to the edge,
I'm glad I didn't fall to Vlad the Impaler,
I had to lose some sensation,
So I can remain sensational,
Becoming numb in hopes of combating neurosis.

I'm a little rough along the edges,
As the ceiling is falling down on me,
The higher it gets,
The stronger the foundation has to be.

Abruptly pulling the curtain down,
For I do not want my radiance to be sapped,
Since luminous leeches are all across the audience,
To be sapped or zapped,
That is the question,
Searching for that third outcome,
Constricted by the false dilemma.

Chrome Flowers

Technology is a metric of our advancement as a species,
Becoming a more developed society,
The margin of error becomes ever-increasingly smaller,
Technology is often misused and abused by us,
Leading to inventions that create sour results,
Resulting in the human wrath,
The more civilization seems to progress,
The more we risk deviating away from our true nature,
Eventually reaching the point of no return.

In the Stone Age the population's demise was dependent on the environment:
From ice ages to volcanoes to comets,
Now we have a million ways to cause our own termination,
Along with the general ecosystem as a whole,
We are no longer nurturing ourselves or other life forms.

The disconnect starts at the individual level,
For even if I spend brief moments overindulging myself,
In the myriad of technological devices at our disposal,
I feel like I am wasting my life.

Ambush

I have a date with destiny,
Which fell on deaf ears,
As she gave me the kiss of death,
Now fate has picked up my corpse,
To finish the deed,
When I once held the lead.

To their astonishment,
I gravely rose,
As if from the grave,
With a look of astronomical agitation,
Never taking into account such resolve,
Fear suddenly strikes them both,
Making their sudden escape,
Now I maniacally grin,
So used to lurking in the depths,
Where the fallen reside,
This guest is now festering,
Plotting to annihilate,
What originally caused him to hate.

Chapter 4
Tribulation

Elemental Grasp

How do we handle the challenges, rigors, and setbacks bestowed upon us?
It involves the use of the four elements,
For we are just tiny cells in the body of the Earth,
And operate under certain cosmic laws,
Under rules as fundamental as gravity.

Retain and cultivate the **fire** inside,
And keep it alive no matter how small the ember gets,
For it will not only provide you warmth and guidance,
But with the passion and zest to bring out your best,
This fire will fuel you under the harshest conditions,
However, if it runs out, you'll be in a cave without the proper light.

Stick to your roots on the **earth** through all the turbulence,
Maintain your grounding in order to survive the pounding,
For the daily grind takes a massive toll on the mind,
Without a firm foundation one is bound to falter,
Like stepping into quicksand,
Staying centered despite the 360-degree rotations,
Is key to withstanding the gyrations,
Maintaining the strength of a stone,
Keeps you secure to the bone.

Emulating the adaptability of **water** is a must,
After all our bodies are mostly comprised of it,
We need the ability to adequately respond to any situation,
While retaining our true selves in the process,
Just as water seamlessly transitions into three different states,
While keeping its molecular composition intact,
For in the animal kingdom it is not the fittest who survive,
But the most flexible to change as a direct response to external stimuli.

Harnessing the power of the **wind** through your vocals is crucial,
To express one's ideas and concerns to others advances our species,
Leading to new inventions and breakthroughs,
Just as a newborn screams in order to be fed,
Speaking up is deemed necessary to make sure needs are met,
It also contains the power to captivate audiences,
Effective speakers make their voices transform the globe,
By bestowing on the minds of the masses the trait of possibility,
All carried through tiny vibrations that echo through the air.

Master these four elements within your core,
To be set up for splendid results,
Suddenly, insurmountable obstacles will appear obsolete,
You will delete old paradigms that chained up progression,
To develop newfound skills that will lessen corrections.

Petri Dish

I'm trapped inside a container,
In the same scenario bacteria multiply exponentially,
Yet I'm stuck in the exact same spot,
No growth or development whatsoever,
There are nutrients, water, and air to keep me alive,
That's about it though, seems very anti-climactic,
I take a look past the container,
And see pairs of eyes peeping at me,
"How bizarre," I think to myself.

Could it be that this whole life...
I've been nothing but a science experiment in action?
What is the hypothesis that has been conjured about me?
This must be a double-blind study,
Since I've been oblivious this whole time,
If I escape these confines,
Will I be able to resist and persist?
Or will antibodies just swallow me up?
Will the lack of structure unravel me like dismantling a quilt?
I'm not sure whether this environment is keeping me alive or inhibiting me,
Or maybe both.

Table Scraps

Malnourished in affection,
Embraced by hardship,
Smothered by adversity,
Smooched by catastrophe,
Enduring it all,
The tough love,
As time passes,
Embracing the fast,
Used to last,
Place in race,
Turning my face,
Little too late.

Starvation forged me,
Look at this:
What I developed,
What I created,
What I became,
It makes sense,
Now I learned,
That this was,
In my case,
The only way.

Maquiladoras

There is an epidemic of illness around,
An endemic occurrence that happens in the metropolis,
The hospitals keep piling up with people,
Autopsy reports are filling up at an increasing rate,
We are misled to run a 100-meter dash on a triathlon.

We keep getting bombarded by stress,
Like being thrust into an asteroid belt,
Only to get ferociously plummeted in all directions,
And get astonished,
When the stress fractures leave us demolished.

We are taught to work harder,
To the point of collapse,
Instead of smarter,
Where all the different factors are optimized,
To hit the sweet spot of productivity.

The response usually comes when it's no longer effective,
Fiddling with our health for the attainment of wealth,
The tension ends up eating us from the inside like a parasite,
Misleading us in the search of a sacred site,
Until one day we end up realizing,
That we were trained while half-asleep,
To mass-produce Model T's,
Being discouraged and ridiculed for taking that big leap,
Transforming into cheap labor,
In this company called freedom,
Exporting our end result to who knows where.

Chaos everywhere
Create your luminescence
Code reality

Resilience

One of the most important yet underrated traits,
Resilience is the defiance of a disintegrating silence,
Winners are forged by surviving the chisel,
Sculpted into a Michelangelo masterpiece,
Admired by even the angels,
A splashing of the paints is commonplace,
But one must not let it become the defining feature,
Even primary colors are secondary to the true form of the sculpture,
The core buried underneath a layer of thin meaning,
For if the interior cracks,
The reverberations will crumble the statue,
An excess of pillars may have ugly form,
But the priority is keeping the building around.

Chambers

Need to work with the papyrus,
While sustaining myself on papayas,
Scriptures must be changed with new scrolls,
This is the decree of the pharaoh.

Undergoing massive projects,
A modern-day Ramses II,
Along with massive campaigns,
In the scale of Thutmose III.

In search of grandeur,
The obelisk shows me the way,
Seeking my own place,
In the valley of Thebes.

Doctor T.J. Eckleburg glares at me,
In the form of the Sphinx,
As the tombs reveal their secrets,
A new dynasty has begun.

The flooding makes wheat and barley,
As I'm able to hang on, barely,
These tribulations start to take their toll,
Bennu lend me your strength!

To be able to make it out,
From the heaps of ashes,
Is the end of time upon us?
Where everything just fades away?

Can't succumb to this thinking,
Under captivity I must arduously carry stones,
Across vast distances,
To build the pyramids.

Recipe

The trauma is too much to deal with,
I have to put up with all this dogma,
A hiatus is much needed,
To be removed from the picture,
A temporary lessening of panic,
To sit back, contemplate, and regroup,
In order to plan for the epic coup,
And stir up the ingredients in the soup.

Only problem is,
That I don't know the formula that's needed,
I ceaselessly worry about overcooking,
Or not preparing it well enough,
What if I need to cook another dish entirely,
And all that effort was for naught?
In the process I become distraught,
Resorting to bake a cake from scratch,
But removing the sugar,
Since my results are nothing short of disgusting,
Retuning the mechanics for a last stand,
Encrusting a layer of pure grit,
Perhaps I went about this all wrong,
Forgetting to make a cookbook,
And letting the eating blocks slip,
Through every nook and cranny.

Progression

Disgusted by my emaciated figure,
I enroll in the iron city of the gym,
And start to relish this place,
These sets and reps,
Are the antidote to reset.

I enter full of vigor and motivation,
And leave full of pains and aches,
Progressively adding the weights,
Obsessively tracking my progress,
Eating like a Viking to replenish the calories,
Sleeping like a sloth to repair the damaged muscle fibers,
Emerging slightly stronger and more fit each time.

Eventually obligations interfere,
Ceasing to work out,
My newfound muscular frame shrinks,
Which has me feeling frail,
Since I'm back to square one,
Learning this isn't a one-and-done deal.

Discipline

To maintain discipline becomes all the more elusive,
Becoming a disciple of the merry-go-round,
Digging myself deeper into a Mariana Trench,
With too much force that prevents a departure to the surface,
This leads to being curled up in the corner of my room,
Trapped in the bottom of a slide,
Unable to get off the easy way,
Instead just helplessly climbing up,
Only to slide back down,
Each and every time.

The schedule becomes evermore constricting,
Have I picked the wrong routine to begin with?
I'm all-in, doubling down,
Or so I think?
Because I've only ended up in the land down under,
Is it the result of some boomerang effect?
Organizing sections of a binder is so easy,
But transferring that outside the paper turns into a jumbled mess.

Shopping Spree

Supervisors that go on power trips,
Mistakenly believing themselves superior,
When they're actually a bunch of imbeciles,
Backstabbing workers like Roman politicians,
Thinking they're hot stuff like they own the Louvre,
When they have a minimal education in all aspects,
No loyalty since they're not reciprocal towards their subordinates,
Our noble efforts are returned with—
Threats, insults, and excessive criticism,
And they wonder why the company culture breeds cynicism,
Managers that can't even properly manage their emotions,
Let alone an entire store.

Employee training is always pushed back,
Framing and setting us up for failure,
Learning on the job is needed for survival,
Throwing us into the pit of the savannah,
To deal with entitled princess shoppers like Hannah,
Cleaning departments only for a tornado of hands to leave ruins,
Manager, you expect me to face every aisle solo,
When you don't even lift a finger yourself?
This leads to forming compartments of fury,
As we extend our closing shift to clean up the mess.

Seasons are artificially constructed to keep up with the demand,
Supply me with some entertainment,
To help me cope with the brash consumers,
And they wonder why I'm fuming to the brim on the job,
The defective items pile up like a wasteland,
With more inefficiency than a contraband,
Corrective measures from the higher ups only make things worse,
The operations process is a mess,
Call this black ops,
This whole situation has become topsy-turvy,
And all of this nonsense for just the minimum wage.

Alchemist

Throughout the eons people have been searching,
Seeking to capture the power of chemical merging,
To turn "ordinary" elements into something of value, such as gold,
Perhaps that is attributed to greed,
Which leads to the committing of malignant deeds,
All in the hopes of rearranging infinitesimal atoms.

The most potent and reverential form of alchemy,
Is not the transforming of elements into a precious metal,
But turning one's pain, sorrow, and hardships into something productive,
It is to resist implosion and to use the otherwise lethal flares,
To create an ongoing beacon of radiance,
That brings warmth and inspiration to all around.

One can either burn his or her life away in a swift blaze,
Like a supergiant star using all of its fuel,
Destroying itself in a chaotic symphony,
Or use one's fuel more conservatively,
Like a red dwarf star,
That can last indefinitely,
To accomplish one's voyage,
Using efficient energy conversion as the basis,
And to stack negativity, misfortune, and sorrow,
Into the personal nuclear cores,
Like fuel in an engine,
To forge a form of alchemy,
That simultaneously turns you into an unstoppable force and an immovable object.

Momental Advantage

The pendulum is in my favor,
Though this type of challenge I learned to savor,
Not falling for the vertigo of oscillation,
String theory is the only thing keeping me together,
Titillation moves me back,
Disgust moves me forward,
Horned creatures charge me under heresy,
My response is that I'm here to stay,
To love pity halts the velocity,
Sin city is covered under a veil,
What's supposed to be the final nail in the coffin,
Now finally turns out to be the bail,
Pivoting between motion and being inert.

The tarot determines the value of the karat,
At least that's what I'm told,
Don't need a crystal ball to see through the dealer's poker face,
Pouting and stalling won't get me a better draw of cards,
The bling won't let me take matters into my own hands,
Although blind to the next course of action to take,
I can't waste the momentum,
A final fling is the best response,
Hoping that the calculations are my lover.

Stuck

Thrust into the unrelenting depths,
Heading towards a way out,
Tiptoeing through the scorching landscape,
Although the pain is excruciating,
I've been trained to escape this jail by timid trepidation,
Instead of instinctually sprinting to escape the peril,
Looking behind my back at every moment,
The paranoia kicks in at high gear,
Causing a malfunctioning of my components,
Until I break apart like a used watch.

Engineering an outpost into the outermost reaches of the sky,
Upon completion it becomes apparent that there is no going back,
Stranded on a floating island,
The stars appear closer within reach than ever before,
However, my inclination is to avoid cutting my feet,
While walking on pieces of glass,
Left stranded in a vacuum of thin air,
Failing to find a way to pierce the atmosphere,
And make my entrance into the doorstep of the heavens.

Chapter 5
Purgatory

Trifecta

A place littered with gleaming beaches.
That stays hidden under the table.
Like me, you are under the radar.
Where arts and crafts flourish.
An old western touch filled with Spanish influence.
My coronation began here.

This area is perceived as the middle of nowhere.
But underneath this dirt patch,
Lies a rural and cultural metropolis.
The best seafood in the world is enjoyed here.
The residents drink beer so carefree,
And the community is tight-knit like a tribe.
The decorated mountain of memories oversees the inhabitants.

Although I wasn't born here,
You welcomed me in your arms as one of your own.
The quirky and startup capital of the world.
Where techies make their nest.
Although the skyscrapers are not the biggest here,
The innovation is unparalleled.
Like the companies here,
I build myself up from the very bottom.
An extremely prideful culture that undoubtedly rubs off on me.

You've all helped make me who I am today.
As distinct as you each are,
I'm a blend of your individual attributes.
An unlikely and puzzling synthesis,
Forging this individual from scratch.

Torrent

The tears are overflowing,
The emotions are overwhelming,
Call me an overbearing burden or an overload,
But this is more than just feeling a little under the weather,
I was never one to be thick-skinned like leather,
This sensitivity is more like a burden than a gift,
Needing a lift to prevent a massive rift,
All of my liquid is being converted into raindrops.

With enough sadness in me to sustain a tropical rainforest,
It's relentlessly pouring away nonstop,
The levee has broken and the torrent is underway,
Enveloping a field to lay waste to the crops,
Shield me away from the terror abound,
Or hide me in the depths of a mound.

I need a thunderstorm to change the mood,
To make me a force to be reckoned with,
A lessening of weakness will serve me well,
The effects of which only time will tell,
My days are sour with the pouring of lime,
To save the day I have to risk destruction,
Ergo it's a roll of the dice I'm willing to take,
Unleashing the hatred in me may be the only way,
An eruption might prevent my sacrifice to Chac,
So I can chalk a victory by balancing both light and dark.

Shards

The trust we once had has become almost nonexistent.
It was shattered into a vast multitude of pieces.
Sadly it becomes much easier to assemble a palace of lies,
Than it is to form a room of honesty.
Our situation appears irreparable,
Which is why I seem inconsolable.
Somewhere in this junkyard of deception,
There is a tiny fragment,
That has the potential to fix everything.
A remedy and repair job of epic proportions.
Although the trust between us is almost gone,
That doesn't mean the love is.
And that force can make our bond stronger than it ever has been.

Distortion

I can't tell the difference between:
The house of mirrors in carnivals and our municipalities.
Everything is artificially constructed in our urban setting,
And just like the former,
Is made of nothing but glass,
In that the fragility is ever-present,
Things are so easy to break and crumble,
That no one can even tell that they were made by people in the first place.
No matter how far I traverse in the house of mirrors,
I see nothing but illusions,
Just particles of light that reflect off of even surfaces.
Similarly society is just smoke and mirrors,
You look at the lens and the collections have no meaning,
Except the meaning that we place upon them.
And just like the carnivals,
Where you have to be alert for scary clowns,
You need to be on the constant lookout,
For clowns that ruin your daily affairs.
In these types of fairs and in society,
You also win tickets based on your merit,
In order to earn prizes.

The Great Depression

My Great Depression,
Similar to the one that devastated the nation,
Except I didn't go through the Roaring Twenties,
There's no stimulus package to raise me up,
I turn to look up and see my cabinet as empty as a shelf,
Down so low I feel like a sullen elf,
So distraught by the giant dust bowl I'm stuck in.

I don't see the way to raise my stock,
So I make like a bird and just flock,
Climbing up an endless hill,
Maybe I'm just too soft and need to win the war,
Not a global one that needs gore,
But one in my perimeter,
Where I control the door,
And can survive the harsh shore.

Covalent Bonds

My electrons have been stripped from me,
Valence has been turned into valet,
Twirling me around and around like a ballet,
Hijacking my original chemical composition,
The result is the formation of cyanide,
As I say sayonara to my treasured blueprint.

What appears to be an easy fix,
Is really an atomic farce,
There is no way to comprehend the totality of this mess,
I believe there is one level to this,
But there are actually layers of rings revealed,
Orbiting around me,
Forming an unbreakable knot,
As I alternate between different realities and scenarios,
Where the perception ends up blinding me,
And the vision becomes overwhelming and binding.

I search for a chemist to find freedom from this bond,
To conjure up a solution from a test tube,
Even if I turn into a science test dummy,
Knowing that the results may turn out crummy,
For either I will strip away from the compound,
With all the particles I started out with,
Or I will be completely vaporized,
In a molecular breakdown.

Waitlisted

Striving for commencement is the objective,
To kill off procrastination and conclude the odyssey,
Standing in my way are certain courses,
Acting as gatekeepers towards the completion of my journey,
Even gaining access to sign up for them is a roadblock,
The open spots are few and far between;
I just sit there begrudgingly waiting,
These core classes leave me mentally sore,
Unable to add them — denies me the blocks to build a skyscraper,
I cannot house this company of grandeur,
As the requirements keep piling up,
Bogging me down in a veil of commitment,
Being out on reserve until I'm lost,
In the middle of no-man's-land,
This school of hard knocks deconstructs my Fort Knox,
With no tactics to strategize on the battlefield,
Resulting in a losing fight from the start,
Leading me to realize,
That the placeholders and external combatants,
Were never the decisive factor,
If my institution failed me,
Then it was up to me,
To either transfer to a more promising campus,
Or slip my way through the system,
To obtain the coveted degree of victors.

Noteworthy

Dear 10-year-old me,

I'm deeply sorry for letting you down.
For not living up to your expectations.
For giving in when we were right at the cusp of a breakthrough.
For not fighting tooth and nail for what we believe in.
For not training harder, and putting in more work.
For allowing others to dictate the course of our lives, and not ourselves.
For neglecting your heart,
and choosing the safe and complacent route.
For ceasing to believe in miracles.
For growing bitter and resentful.
For locking you in a prison,
In the confines of my subconscious mind.
I don't know if I have it in me to turn this around.
I've fought so many battles that I'm spent.
The only feasible way I can see a resolution is:
If I let you take full control of my being.
But I'm scared of what would happen.
Of the outcome.
Of crashing and burning.
Maybe that is why,
I was bound to fail in the first place.

Lamentably,

_____

Multi-Tool

My thermometer has plummeted,
Body temperature is cooling,
So I recoil while the shivers kick in.

My barometer has skyrocketed,
I end up folding and squishing as a result,
For the pressure is too much to handle.

The field is disturbed,
And it renders my compass useless,
Leaving me to fretfully wander,
With no direction or purpose.

The only thing I have that functions,
Is my handy pair of binoculars,
But it is of no use to me,
As I traverse the cave,
Where the abyss envelops me.

Amnesia

Blank slate with a lack of responsiveness,
Can't seem to remember what brought me here in the first place,
With an inability to make a self-assessment,
I lost my very own scouting report,
So I resort to pouting,
The channel to my own wisdom is blocked.

Wondering if jogging the memory is even viable, let alone worth it,
A crucial segment of my past is locked away,
Like a misguided relic that never found its way to the sanctuary,
Reinvention is the ultimate form of empowerment,
Yet endowing one's self with the proper guidebook provides an underrated advantage,
Such as a lighthouse leading a lost ship to land,
Sometimes it's best to forget,
Other times, it's necessary to remember,
In order to grab the bull by the horns,
Before you get knocked off the ride.

Monster

My whole life I've been seeing you as the monster.
Who has been preventing me from going after my dreams.
Constantly scolding me and putting me down with destructive criticism.
Breaking me down until I lose my sense of worth.
Frightening me with your unexpected bursts of anger.

So I retreat like a hermit,
And just stay in my shell,
Resulting in me being shell-shocked.
Being drained of the desire to live,
And the desire to be free.

Then one day,
I realized that all along,
The monster was not you, but me.
I was *the* monster for my venomous resentment,
Not knowing that holding grudges can put smudges on the soul.
I was too proud and resentful to forgive you.
When you grew up overcoming such a rough childhood.
Putting up with mistreatments of all kinds,
Yet developing the strength to overcome all of that.
Strength that I misunderstood as heartlessness.
When it was the exact opposite.

As a grown man you decided to leave your country,
And immigrated to the states.
Leaving behind a life of extreme poverty and misery,
As you realized that even with a master's degree,
You didn't have many opportunities in your land.
You came to America without a single cent,
And a wife and two kids to provide for,
One of them being me.
Somehow you became a living example of the American Dream.
Working two jobs for many years,
Getting by on four hours of sleep a night or less.
And learning the English language,
Without a need for classes or teaching materials.

Fast-forward to today and you're not only well-established,
With a career many born here would struggle to attain,
But you've also become a successful entrepreneur.
I grew up sleeping on the floor, under tables.
While you starved yourself to make sure I was fed.
Now we live well, in a great home.
You even managed to pay for my entire college education, every last cent.

And here I'm bitching over petty and minuscule matters,
Especially compared to the things you've had to deal with.
I never took accountability for seizing my life,
And turning my visions into a reality.
Instead I blamed you, when 100% of it was supposed to go to myself.

For wanting to hurt you out of spite,
With my passive-aggressiveness,
Constantly giving you the cold shoulder,
I'm the monster.
It might be too late for an apology on my part now.
But I hope I'm able to right my wrongs,
For the way I hurt you.
In fact, all I've ever wanted out of life,
Apart from accomplishing my soul's mission...
is to make you proud.

Torture Room

The quarters of punishment left painful remnants.
Where shrieks pin-balled inside the walls.
And innocence was traded for acrimony.
Memories were stretched to the point of breaking,
As if vigorously yanking film.
So many days, months, and years are spent here.

Eventually the sacrificial chamber is converted into a venerable space.

What once broke the spirit,
Now conditions and strengthens the will.
Fury cools into the granite of insight.
Artifices of hatred become seen as trivial trinkets.
A place that's hated is now relished.
Seen as a rite of passage.
The initiation ritual was passed with flying colors.

Event Horizon

An accident has left me severely injured.
The ambulance transports me at full speed.
I'm at a hospital bed, on the border between life and death.
The screen goes flat, as doctors frantically rush to attempt to revive me.

Suddenly, I'm teleported into the vacuum of space.
A force starts tugging at me,
Pulling me into its grasp.
I get sucked into this force,
Leaving me spaghettified.
On the accretion disk appears a collage of my own memories.
I see random snippets of my different life experiences,
That are out of order,
Which leaves me to structure the pieces together.

I see my entire life pass by in just moments.
I see where I make my biggest perceived mistakes,
Along with all the missed opportunities.
I notice all the different times people have harmed me,
Along with every occurrence where I harmed someone else.
I also see different courses of results,
From alternate decisions I would have taken in other timelines,
Or decisions I never took altogether — that I made in my current life.

Throughout this process streams of information leave the multitude of images
surrounding me,
And get enveloped into me,
Where I learn vital information,
That far exceeds the output of all the data in the entire computer age.
I have what seems like millions of tubes of pure data,
Plugging into my body,
Until I'm filled with the pinnacle of wisdom.

When this whole process is done,
I get spit out of the accretion disk like a blazar,
And in a nanosecond end up back in the hospital bed.
Somehow I've not only survived and awoken from my coma,
But I've also made a full and miraculous recovery.
This is my second chance.
I know what I need to do.
No more rest.
I have work to do.

Chapter 6
Salvation

Slice of Paradise

What does it take to reach the upper echelons?
Where victory is fully guaranteed?
Where failure is not even a possibility?
And angels stay blessing you at every corner,
No matter how dim the luminosity around is?

If the lock that seals heaven is located,
How then do you unlock it?
Do you find a locksmith,
To forge you a new pair of keys?
Or pick the lock using a makeshift device,
Like a thief breaking into a car or safe with a simple pin?

Elation may lead to elevation,
Although that sensation is only temporary and fleeting.
A brief lift that takes you to the peak,
Before you go crashing down like Icarus.

Reserves

I have been kicked, battered, tossed, and nearly destroyed by life,
Enduring a never-ending onslaught of pain and turmoil,
My own tank is pointing towards empty with no fuel station in sight,
Where many would perish somehow I am still standing alive,
This must be divine intervention from a higher dimension,
As suddenly a wave of vigor and passion envelops me,
Now I achieve the impossible with herculean feats,
Transforming from a helpless kitten into a mighty lion,
Building the fortitude of a medieval fortress,
Beating the odds against the most rigged casino of all: this world.

El Cielo

Witnessing a play that mirrors the dance of creation.
Joyously splashing in a liquid aurora borealis.
Canoeing across a magical stream,
Covered with a dark blanket that is sprinkled with luminous spots,
Feasting on an exotic delicacy that enamors and seduces the taste buds.
Traversing eons through the exploration of ancient ruins.
Zip-lining through fear in a blazing expedition.
Racing through the heart of the jungle to rediscover myself.
Leaping into the unknown...
Inside a pool of mystery.

Meadows

Once the ruler of a vast empire,
Now this king has faded into obscurity,
Or so people think.
He ruled massive armies with the slightest ease.
His current purpose is to assemble a vascular collection of rulers.
He is their humble subject.
Currency made in his image was spread across the land.
Now he spreads and nourishes a plethora of seeds,
To give back to the land.
He ordered the execution of countless individuals,
Some for the most trivial reasons.
Now his rebirth has revolutionized his core,
As he dreads even the thought of harming a butterfly.

As a monarch he established policies to bring order to his many provinces.
His non-commercial green thumb has taught him:
That true order is upheld by the plants and trees.
All humans must do is mimic their divine nature,
In order to get a taste of the sacred nectar of the gods.
Their stillness is incomparable, even among the worst possible havoc.
Their roots are firmly planted on the ground,
While even the slightest disturbance can destabilize humans.
Their passivity makes them goddesses to emulate.
Ironically, this former king is happier than he has ever been while ruling an empire.
He finds more joy in overseeing the growth of his garden,
Than in the development of city-states, the implementation of laws,
and the subjugation of his subjects.
This man has now become a true king in his right, and in his mind.

Putty

The putty appears as hard as concrete,
When in actuality it's as soft as a pillow,
With it I can build whatever I want,
From a building to a truck to a theme park,
To sharpen my architectural skills,
Opens a whole plethora of possibilities,
There's an endless supply of putty at my disposal,
No reason to steal any away from other builders.

It takes a supreme amount of faith,
To oversee the construction of my design,
Fretting will only lead to a collapse of the components,
Keeping the vision is essential,
Letting anyone else handle the creative process will only lead to a jumbled mess,
When the shape is ready,
All it takes is to glue the formation and let it cement,
Now, all that's left is to celebrate your joyous creation.

Bubble

Ever since childhood my existence has been one of self-preservation,
In a constant tug-of-war to maintain homeostasis,
Amid volatile forces outside of my skin,
Regulating internal health and balance is a central challenge,
Fighting against everlasting centripetal momentum,
Therefore the default state is staying in a passive mode,
The waves are striking and I just want to keep my ship afloat,
These barriers I set are a last-ditch effort to keep myself from bursting,
For if the defenses fall there are no allies in sight to restore my kingdom,
And I have not learned how to repair a demolished edifice,
So I cover myself in plate armor to survive the onslaught,
Though this method of living is constricting and burdensome,
It is the most viable option to make it at the end of the day in one piece.

Righteous

From day one — embracing the correct way,
Being spoon-fed the regulations,
To avoid the cauldron of calamity,
Soaking in information and procedures,
An overspill is unavoidable,
As the conditioning creates a rigid structure,
Until bending the rules becomes unfeasible,
Much less reality,
Constrictions are necessary for order,
Aiding in the proper development,
But an excess ends up depleting the joy,
Forging a standard of nobility and excellence,
Yet bringing about an inner poverty,
Supposed to be living right,
But it feels so wrong.

Loopholes

You don't have to be a lawyer,
To take advantage of the coveted loophole.
There's no set definition for anything.
Language and situations may appear concrete,
But there's always room for varying interpretations.
Tying yourself in knots will only restrict the movement necessary to slip away from
cumbersome situations.
Sometimes one just can't leave it to the grand jury to decide.
There's a difference between being an escape artist and an avoidance artist.
The angle of the trajectory arc can either:
Lead you to strike it rich,
Or become a wasted projectile that can't hit the broad side of a barn.
To know the way out and the way in,
And knowing when to apply each circumstance,
In the appropriate situation,
Makes one exceed the slyness of a con artist,
As the pros and cons are accurately kept,
Like an accountant's balance sheet.

Savior

People have always perceived me,
As some sort of stepping-stone,
Hurting me with their actions and lack of consideration,
Leading to sheer consternation,
As I find a way to regroup.

I'm expected to perform miracles left and right,
Using an unrealistic amount of effort,
To fix people's issues like I'm omnipotent,
When my own dilemmas form a desert of desperation,
With no means to make a treaty demanding reparations,
I keep getting sea salt thrust on me,
Making it even more challenging to remain on the seesaw.

No longer am I a savior for petty matters,
Or a parking lot for unwanted vehicles,
I'm establishing boundaries,
Like the Great Wall of China,
After all these years of being exploited,
Now, I finally know my true worth,
Setting up an enlistment for my own battalion,
Valiantly standing my ground for D-Day.

Latching On

The Buddhists say that attachment leads to suffering;
What kind of attachment does that entail?
Following one's genuine and innermost desires,
Must be an exception to this "rule."
This certainly must differ from going after external vices,
That just serve to fulfill temporary neural connections,
Dopamine rushes leading to false pathways being created in the mind.
Repetition deepens the mental gorges,
Until we become slaves to whimsical mental faculties,
Until your brain ends up schooling you,
All for being unable to pass the classes,
Where you are the only teacher that can grade the criteria.

On the flip side, going after your soul's calling,
Is the best way to avoid living a deceased existence,
Where one's expertise, appetite for self-realization,
and true purpose can be engineered to full completion,
Instead of being cast to the graveyard of expired ambitions.

Divine Companions (Part 2)

A parrot smeared with exotic colors,
A cockatiel who sings his heart out.
Two unlikely companions sharing the same home,
And turning my home into a merry establishment.

Sadly you're locked up in obscurity,
In the very prime of your years.
It becomes a challenge to clean up your constant mess.
And whenever you make noise,
You're covered in blankets to quell you down.
It becomes so easy to take you for granted.

Until, one day, you bid farewell to me.
One leaves, then followed by the other down the juncture.
Was it due to natural causes,
Or something I may have been able to prevent?
Losing my companions has me feeling incomplete.

I wish I was able to care for you better,
And make your existence less miserable.
Am I living life wrong?!
Do I have the wrong ideals in mind?
Are my goals even worthy?
Because I have the premonition that I'm doing something wrong.

Part of me will be counting every moment,
Until I'm reunited with my feathery and furry family,
Sprinting up the stairs of heaven,
Frantically busting the gates open with an unmatched intensity,
After so long, at last, we meet again.
An eternal reunion.
Now nothing will separate us ever again.

Empty

If the universe is operated by energy,
And energy is the ability to do work,
What does that make humans?
Are we just organic wind-up toys?

This has me feeling empty,
But is that the appropriate or ideal state?
The structure of atoms consists of mostly blank space,
And galaxies are spread apart at unimaginably vast distances.

Whenever I feel sad or angry,
I am weighted down like wearing a vest,
Yet joy and love evoke a feeling of elation,
That lifts one above the peat bog of daily and earthly affairs,
Does that mean love and joy are empty as well?
Yet full of genuine meaning at the same time?
The spectrum can make the spectacle burdensome,
But is it the only way true understanding can be achieved?
Piling up the knowledge,
Like fault-blocks elevating mountain ranges.

Instrument

All hope is lost,
Dreams are shattered like broken glass,
No point in maintaining my class,
For there is no honor in going down like this,
It's snowing and clouding the road,
I'm just a pawn in someone else's chess game,
The currents are sweeping me away like I'm a simple prawn.

Suddenly, I'm being led into inspired action,
A presence is taking hold of my operating system,
Not a negative force, but one that feels angelic,
Nourishing me with etheric meals,
So I can make like a businessman and close the deals,
My body is being converted into a divine instrument,
Harmonically playing melodies,
That remedy these ills all around,
Turning me into the illest,
It may seem like my aspirations melt into perspirations,
and escape into thin air,
But maybe this is part of a grander scheme,
Something bigger than myself,
An integral component of a grand orchestra,
To elevate humankind to the top of Mount Olympus.

Genius in a Bottle

I have in my disposition a bottle that can spill genius into the air,
Permeating across the seven continents,
Altering the scope of: the biosphere, lithosphere, and atmosphere.
I closely keep the container with me,
Protecting its intellectual property,
Holding a sentimental value towards it,
Knowing I have been bestowed a precious gift.
Instead of keeping the antithesis of Pandora's box sealed,
For the benefit of the kingdom, I need to release it.
Especially since I've regained leadership,
By reclaiming the crown.
I'm viewed as a psychopath,
When in reality I'm just crazy enough,
To take the route no one else conceives of.
The conception was thanks to camp,
For the sprouting of my ideas, there's no need for contraception.
Only I possess the treasure map for the bottle,
Which I will gladly share with the masses.

Chapter 7
Genesis

Child of the Stars

Never felt like I belonged on Earth.
As long as I remember I've been cast aside as a strange foreigner,
Perhaps it's my innate quietness or lack of fitting in,
Or my bland mannerisms,
For this is a world where the savage brutes dominate,
And perhaps I am too tender,
Being publicly exiled is a phenomenon that is all too familiar to me.

I look up at the night sky and see my true home,
I am a child of the stars with a regal presence,
Seeded on this planet to bring about a massive shift,
Akin to a fifth horseman of the apocalypse,
Who uproots and destroys this wicked establishment,
To usher in a new era of peace and prosperity,
Do not be fooled by this apprehensive demeanor,
Since underneath lies a warrior and revolutionary born to do great things,
I am leaving my mark in an environment so dark,
With a brilliance akin to the brightest quasars in the cosmos,
This youth is achieving legendary feats,
With all the probabilities overwhelmingly stacked against him,
By rewriting the history books with acts of magic.

Mad Scientist

I'm here to answer the calling,
I must hit the lab.
Seeing the tools I have at my disposal to construct.
What invention will I create next?
That can progress humanity?
Rolling this plan out on a giant scale,
Cognizant of the fact that this can either go two ways:
Total destruction or a step closer to utopia.

A device that's make-or-break,
That will either elevate or stagnate.
Tomorrowland is nonexistent,
So I must be willing to unleash madness!
What is the threshold of the cost to pay for this?
Is it better to mitigate the experiment,
In the hopes of preventing widespread destruction?
Or are these steps deemed necessary—
To replace a system that is inherently flawed?

The outcome greatly depends on whether or not the invention reaches
the wrong hands,
So it's hidden from their grasp.
Perhaps the end justifies the means.
The boundaries of morality are blurred,
Like smoke encompassing the Oracle of Delphi.

The razing or the toppling of civilization...
Depends on decisions like this.
Somebody has to make the choice,
Fearing to end up becoming distorted in the process.
It seems too late to turn back.
Unleashing this advancement to society is necessary,
Since it would be a shame for these prodigal powers to decompose like
excess nuclear waste.

Predestined Collapse

Never taken seriously from the start,
Conditioned to reside in the asylum,
Filed away like a classified document,
To fade away in monumental fashion,
All for lack of mental ability,
No recognition for lack of cognition,
The packaging is neat and pristine,
Though the contents are primitive,
Too young to take it all in,
Trained to never go all in,
Seems like it's all etched in marble,
Nothing to really marvel at,
Just a deformed figurine,
Who should be blasted to smithereens,
What fall from grace is that,
If he was portrayed as a worthless gnat.

Polarization

Electric motion is the driving force,
That allows you to cultivate with magnetism,
To blend in uniformity works wonders for self-preservation.
Oftentimes, becoming the solvent does not lead to the solution.
To exhibit the extremes can leave a person a wide-open target.
Such as a magnet, that draws metal to strike it.
Due to containing two opposing charges.

A double-edged sword owning the polarities,
Can draw the most criticism and attack,
Yet also create the field to power the "magnet."
Along with protection from certain types of radiation,
Creating a type of auric field,
Shielding one from criticism, negativity, and anger from others.
It takes a special breed to flip this switch on and off,
As a response or planning ahead in relation to external stimuli.
To alternate between a chameleon,
And a living tumultuous toroidal field.

Statistics

I am grim but not mean,
Being way above average.
Since I'm the middle child,
The median applies to me,
However that does not signify,
That I'm the middle of the pack.
As I get on my mode,
You better move out of the way,
If you don't want to get bulldozed,
As I find the way to replicate results.
Whatever I set my sights on,
I aim to achieve.
This individual is one of a kind,
Quickly raising the z-score,
Only the utmost excellence is for me.
Perfection is what I expect from myself.
A deviation that's not standard,
Since I don't run with the rest of the pack,
That is for squares,
I don't root for the mundane.

Numbers are important since they tell part of the story.
But at the end of the day they don't define me.
I've been a statistical anomaly ever since birth,
And I intend to keep it that way.

Redemption

My dues are finally paid,
Responsibilities are optimally fulfilled,
My every whim and desire is satisfied,
The dim contrast is reversing,
Until the brightness radiates all around,
Seeps into my very core,
And sublimes these chunks of resentment and bitterness,
Snapping me out of this humongous funk,
Until I feel like I'm reborn.

This is proof that cryonics is not needed,
I have a blank page that I can now rewrite with crayons,
Where I have full control of the final draft,
This is coming from someone who was overlooked in the draft,
I wasn't even picked in the 99th round,
But now I've somehow made it into the league,
Putting up Hall of Fame caliber numbers.

Now I can smile upon the heavens,
Since I've achieved liberty,
With glory abound,
Completing the ultimate rebound.

Substitute

She hates that I spend so much time with you,
As I take you out on our sessions her envy balloons,
After I'm left sore from our activities,
She argues with me that I have no energy left for her,
As I spend entire afternoons with you,
She goes out at night with her girlfriends,
To attempt to get me jealous,
But to no avail,
I prefer to admire your face,
Covered with dirt and mud,
Than to pay attention to her face decorated with makeup,
Your symmetry and delectable geometry,
Are much more appealing to me,
Than the curves on her body,
She ends up leaving me,
But I don't care,
Since I relegated her to the bench long ago,
While you took her starting spot,
Ultimately,
I chose you over her,
In order to become a better player.

Playground

Adventure is seeping inside me,
Outgrowing this structure I've played in countless times,
Loan me a different venue as I take this rehearsal up a notch,
Perhaps I will upgrade my recess by:
Shooting pool — using the planets of the solar system as balls,
Wrestle with Orion so I can win his title belt,
Slam-dunk a star cluster in the hoop of a galaxy's central black hole,
Spin a neutron star like a top, making it revolve hundreds of times per second,
Race the Crab Nebula in a swimming competition,
Swing a bat to hit a comet out of the park and into the stands,
landing on a planet to fill it with life-sustaining ingredients,
Challenge a stream of light to a 40-light-year dash,
Create a fireworks show that lights up the night sky,
Playing hide-and-seek inside a nebula,
Going to the very edge of the universe,
To victoriously and graciously lift it up.

The Ascension

I arrive in a Martian-like area,
Yet strangely this place feels welcoming.
Towering sculptures of rock are embedded on the surface,
Spectacular colors are smeared all across,
Like a divine artist painted on the landscape.
This, coupled with the energy vortex all around,
Makes this a sacred pilgrimage.

Off I go to climb one of these mini-mountains,
Quickly quivering in fear as I am mentally ill-equipped,
The ascension is at a snail's pace.
My motion mimics that of a newborn taking those first steps,
Reluctantly learning to navigate novel terrain,
Complicating simple and basic steps like a telenovela,
I reach somewhere not so near the peak of the rock and take a seat.

What I see next leaves a lasting impression on me:
A view so spectacular that it is forever tattooed in the confines of my mind,
In my peripherals there is a red-orange "ocean" littered with green vegetation,
And a strip of highway where the cars look as small as ants,
Titans of stone are the sentinels of the area.
My perspective is altered as I reach a state of transcendence,
In that moment I didn't feel like a little speck of the universe with minimal importance,
But rather like a deity overseeing the clockwork of creation.
With infinitely loving grace and compassion.
Oftentimes it takes trekking through the most treacherous territories,
To reach the greatest epiphanies and see things with a clear lens.

Mastermind

Plunging myself into the epicenter of catastrophe.
Little did I know back then, that this was all part of the master plan.
To send myself into the depths of the maze blindfolded.
Only to then remove it and run into every dead end possible.
Each setback gaining a nugget of wisdom,
Avoiding the pyrite and completing grand deeds along the way.

This was all meant to happen the way events unfolded.
In order to create the biggest and most miraculous change.
All I had to do was survive,
In order to set the dominoes in motion.
To topple the regime.
Putting myself into the trenches all these years,
It was all just part of the plan.
The true mastermind can break free from any situation.
Maybe this was why I cast myself into the depths of despair,
At the lowest possible point, barring death.

At times I was easily startled and shocked,
Now my nerves of steel temper me,
Stacked with an enormous ability to feel,
I wheel over the tension,
Using the static to power nations like Tesla's tower.
Reverse engineering is the way of the almighty,
This is how the *master plan* is enacted.

Mr. Boring

Never at the centerpiece of the exhibit,
Yet that does not deter him or make him livid,
He is perceived as being dull or even repulsive,
An alienated loser who has his head in the clouds,
Though this turns out to be his greatest asset,
As he soars above the pack and escapes the light pollution,
Standing head and shoulders above the rest.

The axis spins along with numerous revolutions around the Sun,
As events play out to be left in the dust,
It actually serves as the perfect cloaking device,
As he pulls the strings of society from his lair,
Transforming the scope of international affairs,
Evolving civilization with his pure and sole will,
And with a vendetta learns to capture the lion's share,
Redefining the meaning of conquest in awe-inspiring fashion.

Rodeo

I loosen the grip on the reins,
Finally able to relax and enjoy the gallop,
Subsiding like the lessening trots,
I give full autonomy to my steed,
A reversal of roles for once.

It does not matter where I'm going, or why,
Realizing I'm so privileged to emerge a veteran,
To have had a chance to circle the laps,
As many times as I've had.

The final frontier is conquered,
The Wild West is tamed,
Now I throw the sombrero up in the air,
Along with my somber mood,
For the graduation ceremony is complete.

This is no ordinary ride,
But more so a final rodeo,
However I'm seen,
Whether a cowboy or an outlaw,
I've outgrown this phase,
Onto the next frontier,
The next life,
The next stage,
Pushing past the door of the saloon,
Heading off towards the sunset.

Universal Agent

A kid who's sluggish and intricately calculated,
Possessing the body of a millipede,
Yet the mind of a supercomputer.
This is a dichotomy destined for disaster,
Though this turns out to be the perfect combination.

He heeds the instant calling,
Pours heart and soul into perfecting a certain craft.
Once the task is completed,
And the objective is marked,
He abandons whatever he's mastered,
As if he never even did it in the first place.

Fate instructs him to pick up the next activity,
Working out the kinks as he figures it out,
A savant who becomes an expert at it in record time,
Only to hang up the boots,
When the job is done.

This mercurial prodigy is at it once again.

The wormhole led him to another route.

Legacy

He was taken into an alternate reality.
Where the fiery depths of the volcano almost swallowed him whole.
Labeled as incomplete and malfunctioning.
Learning to take unheard of routes just to stay afloat.
Sadness was a constant companion.
Madness — a persistent demon.
Finding strength in the least expected places.
Being crowned by the angels.
Until he rediscovered his stellar origins.
Waking up from his slumber,
And elevating along with the pod.
The work ethic became a blessing and a curse.
Anger resulted in being a costly yet sustaining fuel.
Developing a warmongering mentality.
Resulting in a centrality where his full power was unleashed.
Disturbing, upsetting, and shifting the fabric.
A lone figure who has struggled to tame the beast.
Even though he blew his chance,
Animals were his support and blessing.
Thus shouldering the burden.
No longer seeing it as imprisonment,
But the duty of a space voyager.
Through chemistry he learned to manipulate the setting outside the lab.
Seeing the stakes of the sky-high responsibilities placed upon him.
Viewing the horizon made him remember again.
With no other choice now but to blossom as a natural jewel,
To bypass the onslaught of perils.
Activating the mind to overcome the containment.
Envisioning the way out,
While sparks made him sturdy.
Breaking free from the strings,
By measuring and executing a way out.
Now he diligently handles the work,
Whether he wants to or not,
Whether the personal value is significant or minimal.
Since it is the way to set the foundation,
For future generations.
With wizardry he was able to compress a century's worth of achievements,
Into less than a tenth of a century.

What do you want to leave behind,
Once it's all said and done?
How do you want to be remembered,
Long after taking your last breath?
Will you be another imprint in history?
Or dare to become a seismic shock,
Perhaps even a colossal cataclysm?
Will you be left behind and forgotten?
Or cement your place in immortality?
Can the disaster get you to legendary status faster?

www.ingramcontent.com/pod-product-compliance
Lightning Source LLC
Chambersburg PA
CBHW030132260626
47156CB00008B/2917